Helena Olofsson

The Little Jester

Translated by Kjersti Board

R&S
BOOKS

Stockholm   New York   London   Adelaide   Toronto

A long time ago, when the world was almost a thousand years younger than it is today and jesters were traveling the roads, playing music and performing tricks, there was a large monastery in a city in France.

A group of monks lived in the monastery. They had gone there to pray and to work. The monks grew vegetables and grapes for wine, and they painted beautiful pictures in books that they made.

But the most beautiful picture in the monastery was not in a book. It hung in the church. It was the painting of the Weeping Madonna. Eight times a day, the monks went to the church to pray to the Madonna, who wept over all of the bad things that were happening in the world.

One cold and rainy night, when the monks were in the dining hall eating, there was a knock at the door. The Abbot, who was in charge of the monastery, went himself to open the door.

Outside the door stood a little jester. He was cold and hungry and asked them please to let him in. The Abbot did not like jesters. He told the boy to go away.

At that very moment a monk named Philippe happened to pass by. "Reverend Abbot! Please let the boy come in and warm himself! Please let me give him some soup!" said Philippe.

The Abbot thought for a while. Then he agreed. But he gave Philippe strict orders to show the jester to the door as soon as he had eaten.

Then the Abbot went up to his chamber to study.

Philippe took the boy to the dining hall.

The good-hearted monks found all kinds of tasty food for the little jester. They gave him soup, freshly baked bread, a jug of milk, eggs, cheese, chicken pie, pancakes with honey, fruit compote, and almond cake.

The boy ate until he was so full he could not swallow another mouthful. Then he pushed his plate away and smiled.

The monks were curious about the little jester.

"Are you really a jester?" they asked.

The boy nodded.

"Will you show us some tricks?" Philippe asked.

The boy was happy to oblige. He would put on a real show as a way of thanking the monks for the tasty meal. The boy took his empty soup bowl and, with a flick of the wrist, sent it spinning to the floor. The bowl landed on its edge, and he quickly jumped up on it. He started to balance on the bowl at the same time as he kept rolling it with his feet—as if he had been standing on a wheel.

"Bravo! Encore!" the monks cried.

Then the boy took a flute out of his bag. He played a merry tune while he rolled the bowl, with himself on it, out of the dining hall, through the long, dark hallways, toward the large church. The monks followed him with great excitement.

All the way, up to the high altar of the
church, he rolled. Then he jumped up on it so
that everybody would be able to see him. And he began to
play and dance, juggle, do somersaults, and perform magic
tricks while the monks laughed aloud and clapped their hands.

Up in his chamber, the Abbot was studying. Suddenly
he heard a strange noise. It sounded like music.
Actually—no!—it sounded like someone laughing!
Now it sounded like applause.
The Abbot went to the door and listened. He could
not figure out what the noise was. Finally he
decided to go down and see what the monks were
up to.

The dining hall was empty. The Abbot was very
surprised. He looked in the kitchen, in the
library, and in the dormitory, but there was no
one to be found anywhere. Then he heard the
strange noise again. It came from the church.
The Abbot hurried over.

When the Abbot saw the boy and all the monks up by the altar, he
was furious.

"Philippe, you dunderhead! What have you done?" he shouted. The
Abbot rushed up to grab hold of the little jester and throw him out.

But at that very moment the monks pointed toward the altar and cried, "A miracle! A miracle! Look, a miracle!"

The Abbot looked up at the altar. His face turned white. What was happening was truly a miracle.

The Weeping Madonna was no longer weeping. It was as if an invisible hand had repainted the most beautiful picture in the monastery. The Madonna was smiling—she was almost laughing—as she looked down from her place above the altar at the little jester who had shown her his very best tricks. Then the Abbot realized that he had been wrong in wanting to throw the jester out. He begged the boy to forgive him and said, "Ask something of the monastery! Whatever you ask, we will give you, for you made the Weeping Madonna smile!"

At first the boy did not know what to ask for. He was warm and full, so the only thing he needed for himself was a bed to sleep in. But when he had thought awhile, he said, "I wish that you would welcome everyone who knocks at the doors of the monastery. That you would let them warm themselves and give them something to eat, as you did with me."

The Abbot promised, and he kept his word.

From that day on, the doors of the monastery were always open to jesters, the poor, the homeless, and all the other cold and hungry people who traveled the roads.

And what about the boy?

He continued on his way through the world and became a famous jester. Everywhere he traveled, people gathered around to watch his tricks. He made them laugh and forget their troubles for a while. Sometimes you could hear someone in the crowd whisper, "Look! That's the boy who made the Weeping Madonna laugh!"

Rabén & Sjögren Bokförlag, Stockholm
www.raben.se

Translation copyright © 2002 by Rabén & Sjögren Bokförlag
All rights reserved
Originally published in Sweden by Rabén & Sjögren under the title *Gycklarpojken*
Copyright © 2000 by Helena Olofsson
Library of Congress Control Number: 2001089555
Printed in Italy
First American edition, 2002
ISBN 91-29-65499-8

Rabén & Sjögren Bokförlag is part of P. A. Norstedt & Söner
Publishing Group, established in 1823